Hi, Parents!

Your child's love of reading starts here, with HarperAlley's **I Can Read *Comics*!**

I Can Read *Comics* introduces children to the world of graphic novel storytelling and encourages visual literacy in emerging readers. Comics inspire reader engagement unlike any other format. They ask readers to infer and answer questions, like:

1. What do I read first? Image or text?
2. Why is this word balloon shaped this way, and that word balloon shaped that way?
3. Why is a character making that facial expression? Are they happy, angry, excited, sad?

From the comics your child reads with you to the first comic they read on their own, there are **I Can Read *Comics*** for every stage of reading:

LEVEL 1

Simple stories for shared reading.

LEVEL 2

Engaging stories for children reading on their own.

LEVEL 3

Complex stories for independent readers.

The magic of graphic novel storytelling lies between the gutters. Unlock the magic with...

I Can Read *Comics*!

Visit **ICanRead.com** for information on enriching your child's reading experience.

I Can Read *Comics* Cartooning Basics

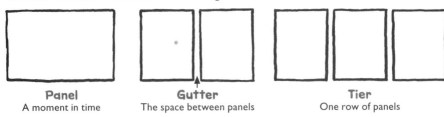

Panel	**Gutter**	**Tier**
A moment in time	The space between panels	One row of panels

Word Balloons When someone talks, thinks, whispers, or screams, their words go in here:

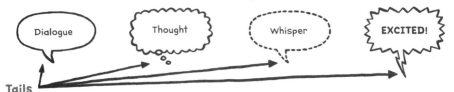

Dialogue · Thought · Whisper · EXCITED!

Tails
Point to whoever is talking / thinking / whispering / screaming / etc.

A quick how-to-read comics guide:

In a **panel**, read the text on the **left** first.

Then, read the text on the **right**.

Remember to...
Read the text along with the image, paying close attention to the character's acting, the action, and/or the scene. Every little detail matters!

No dialogue? No problem!
If there is no dialogue within a panel, take the time to read the image. Visual cues are just as important as text, so don't forget about them!

On a page, **start here**, in the **top left** corner!

After that, read the panel immediately to the **right**.

When you're done up there, come down here and read **this** panel **next**!

ME NEXT! ME NEXT!

You're almost there...

YOU MADE IT! You just read a comic page! YAY!

For my mom and dad —S.W.

HarperAlley is an imprint of HarperCollins Publishers.
I Can Read® and I Can Read Book® are trademarks of HarperCollins Publishers.

Tiny Tales: Shell Quest
Copyright © 2021 by Steph Waldo
All rights reserved. Printed in the United States of America.
No part of this book may be used or reproduced in any manner whatsoever without written permission except in the case of brief quotations embodied in critical articles and reviews. For information address HarperCollins Children's Books, a division of HarperCollins Publishers, 195 Broadway, New York, NY 10007.
www.icanread.com

Library of Congress Control Number: 2021933199
ISBN 978-0-06-306783-7 (trade bdg.) — ISBN 978-0-06-306782-0 (pbk.)

Book design by Joe Merkel
21 22 23 24 25 LSCC 10 9 8 7 6 5 4 3 2 1 ❖ First Edition

LEVEL 3 I Can Read! Comics

Tiny Tales

SHELL QUEST

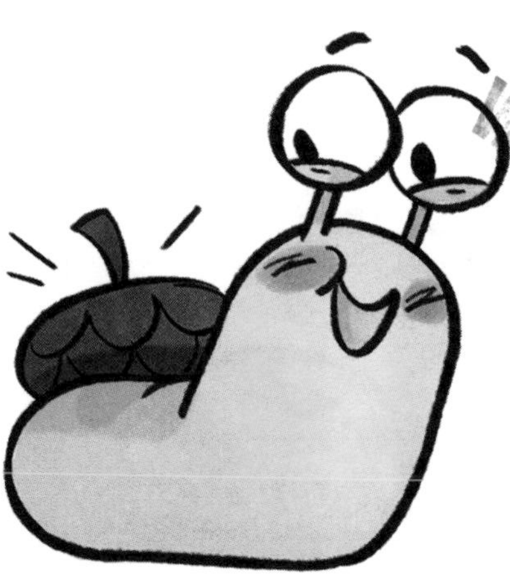

by Steph Waldo

HARPER alley
An Imprint of HarperCollinsPublishers

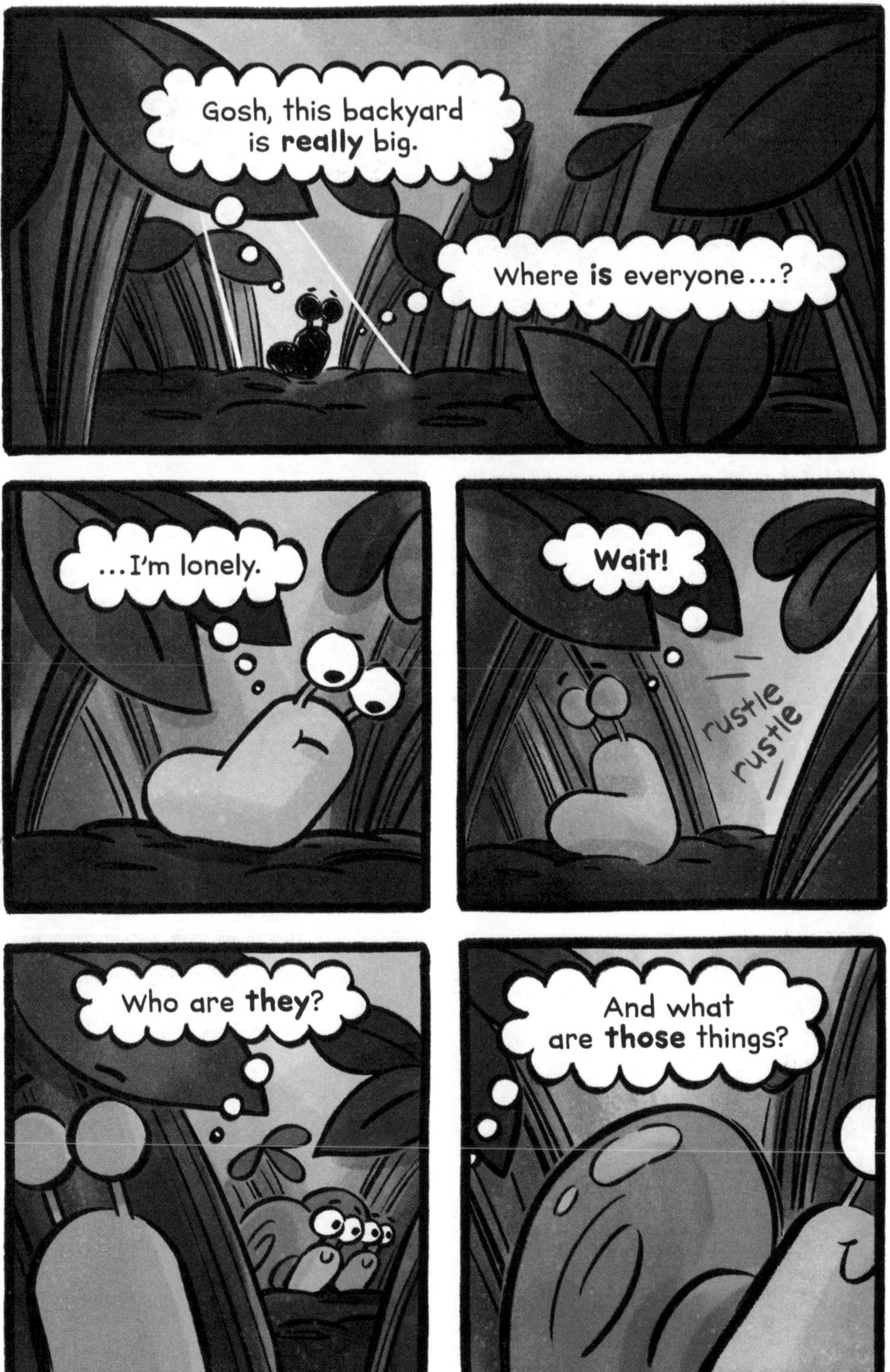
Gosh, this backyard is **really** big.
Where **is** everyone...?
...I'm lonely.
Wait!
rustle rustle
Who are **they**?
And what are **those** things?

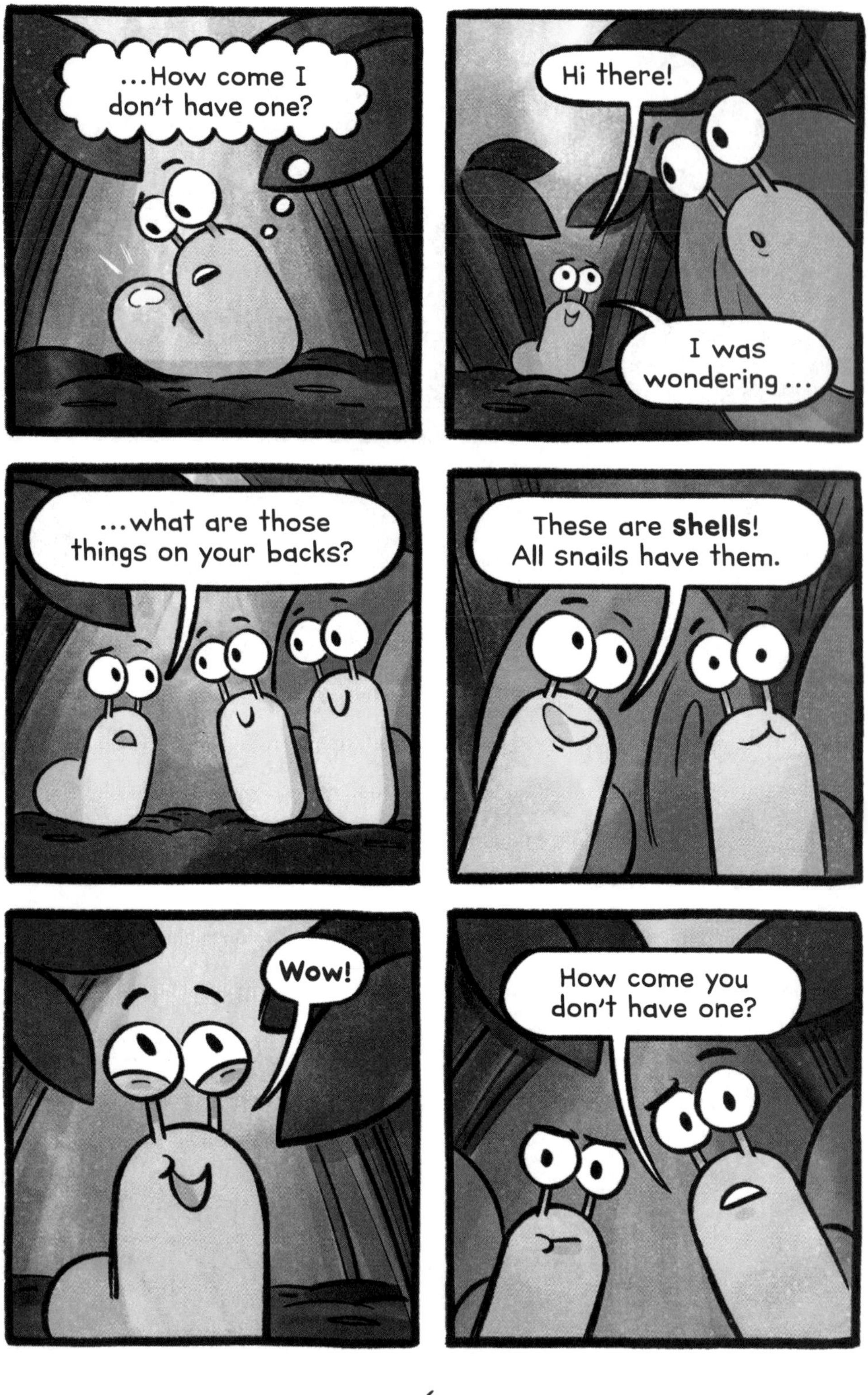
...How come I don't have one?
Hi there!
I was wondering...
...what are those things on your backs?
These are **shells**! All snails have them.
Wow!
How come you don't have one?

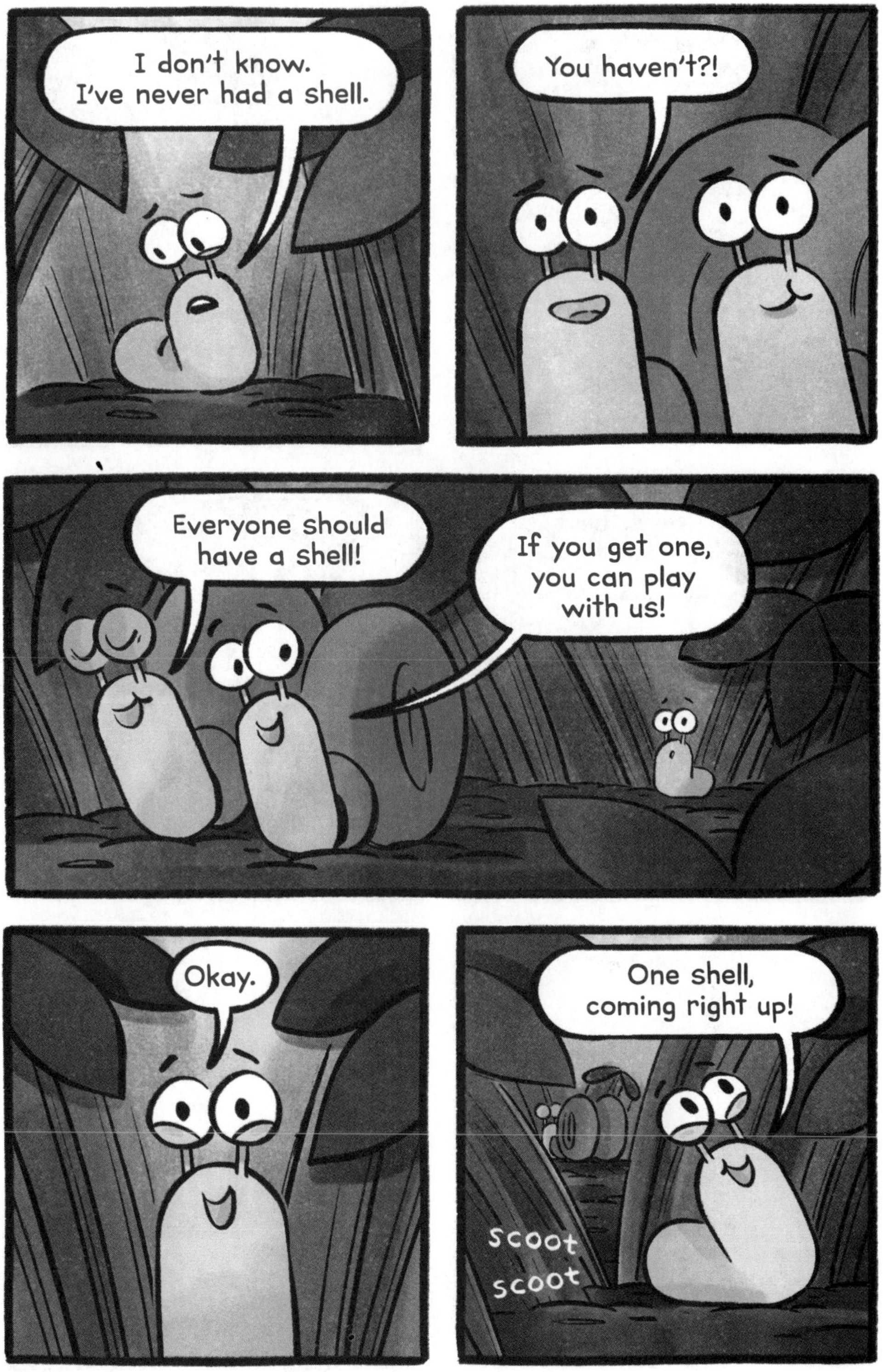

I don't know. I've never had a shell.
You haven't?!
Everyone should have a shell!
If you get one, you can play with us!
Okay.
One shell, coming right up!
scoot
scoot

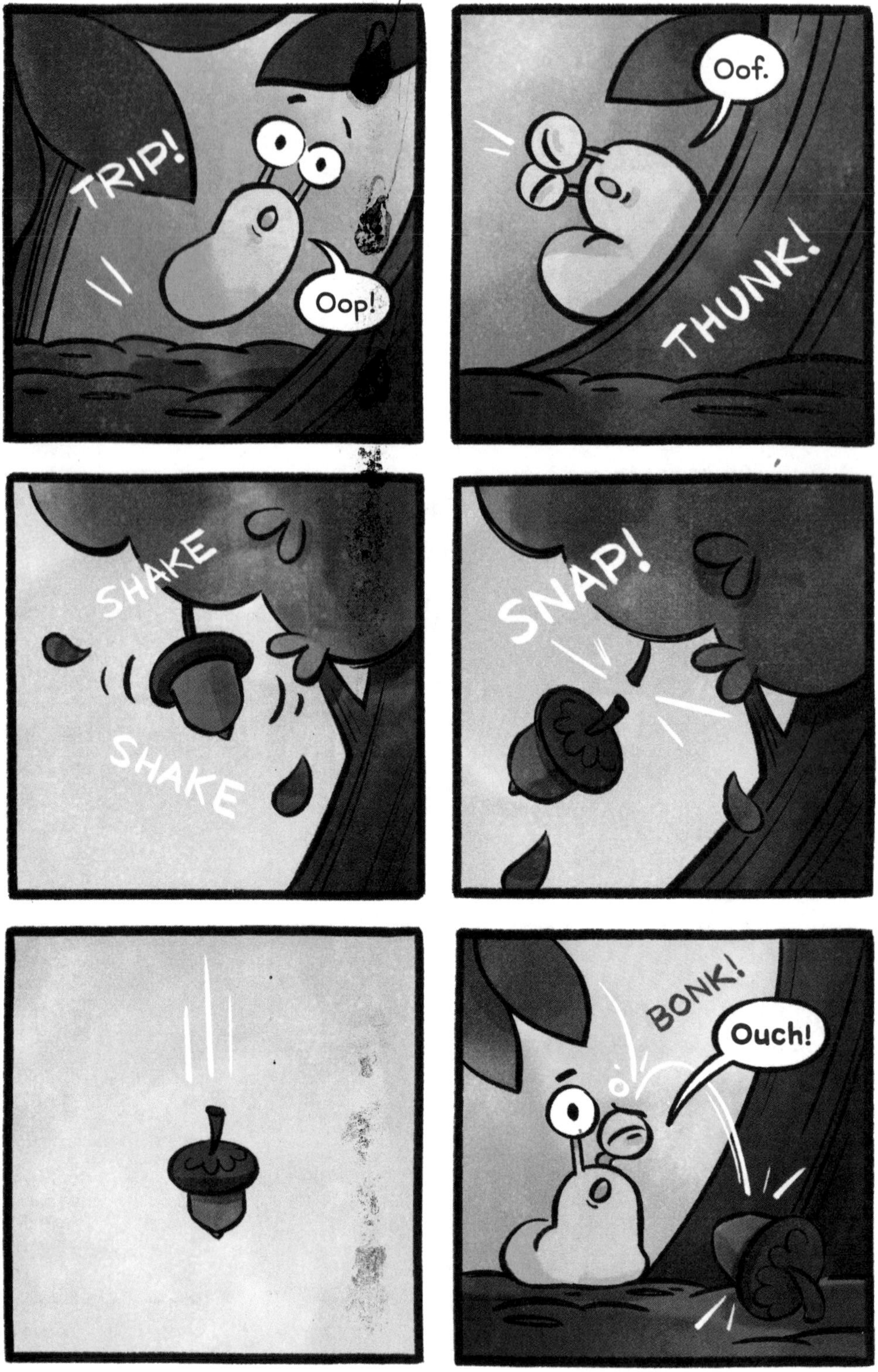
TRIP!
Oop!
Oof.
THUNK!
SHAKE
SHAKE
SNAP!
BONK!
Ouch!

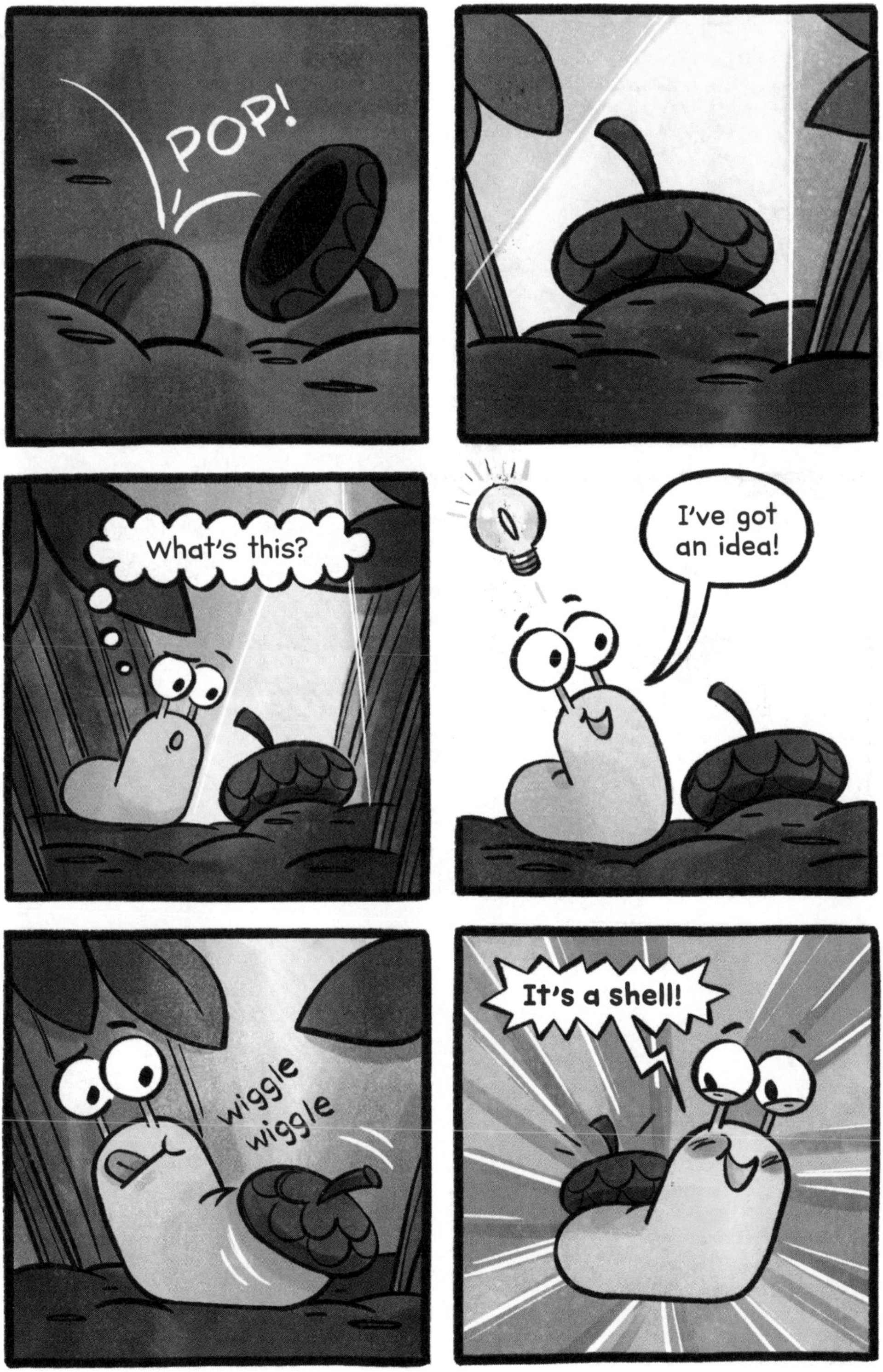
POP!
What's this?
I've got an idea!
wiggle wiggle
It's a shell!

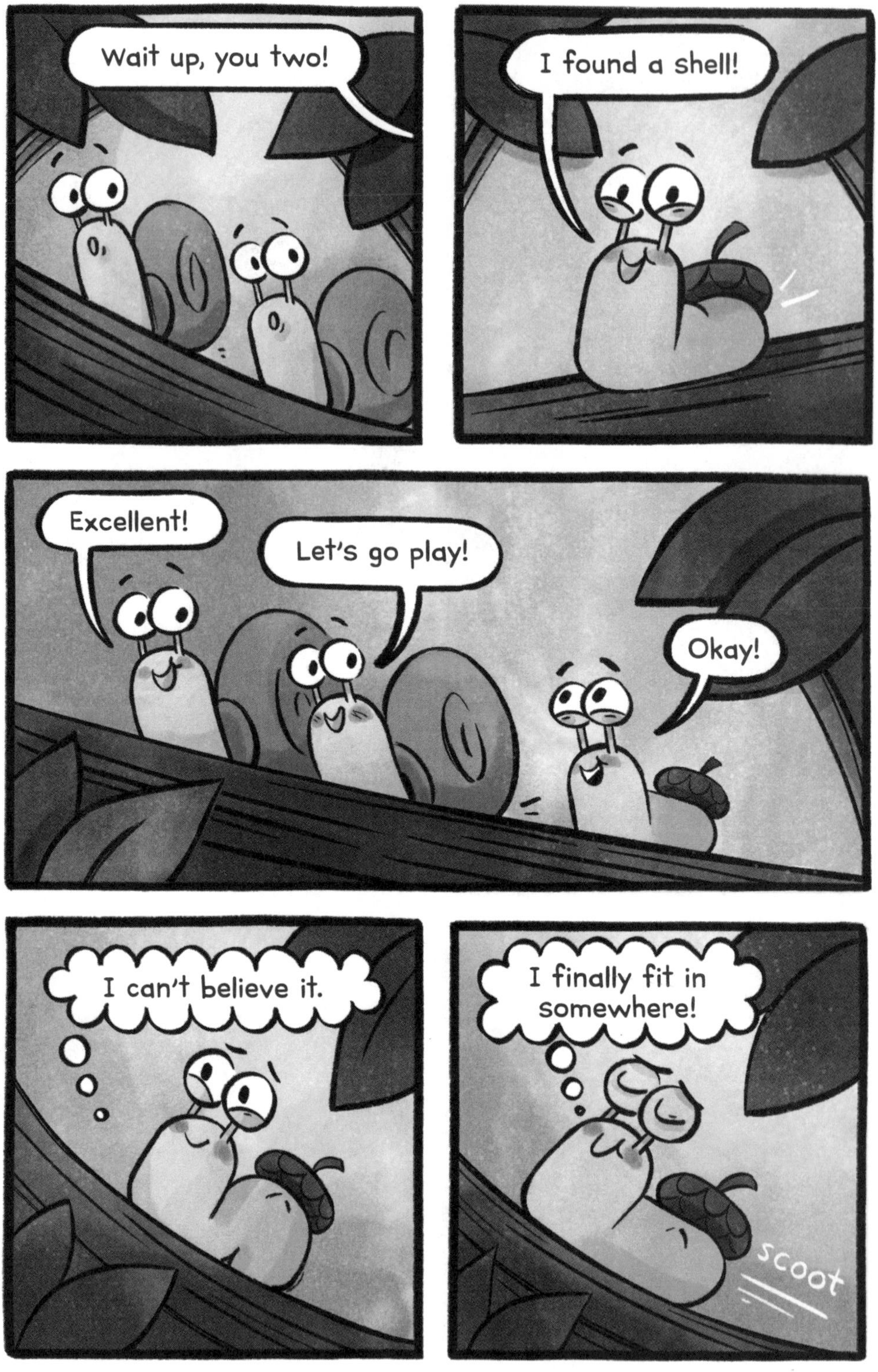
Wait up, you two!
I found a shell!
Excellent!
Let's go play!
Okay!
I can't believe it.
I finally fit in somewhere!
scoot

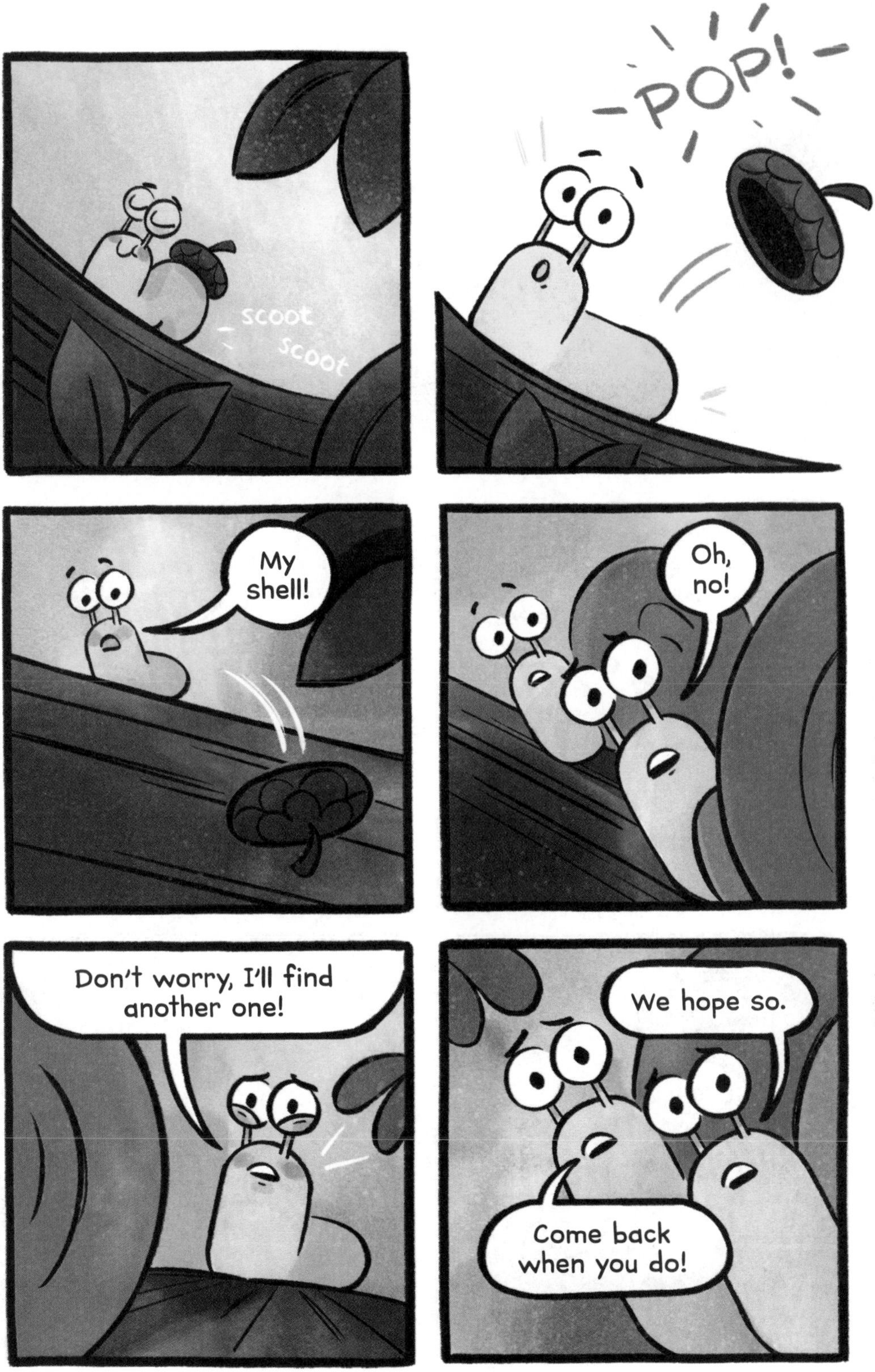
scoot
scoot
POP!
My shell!
Oh, no!
Don't worry, I'll find another one!
We hope so.
Come back when you do!

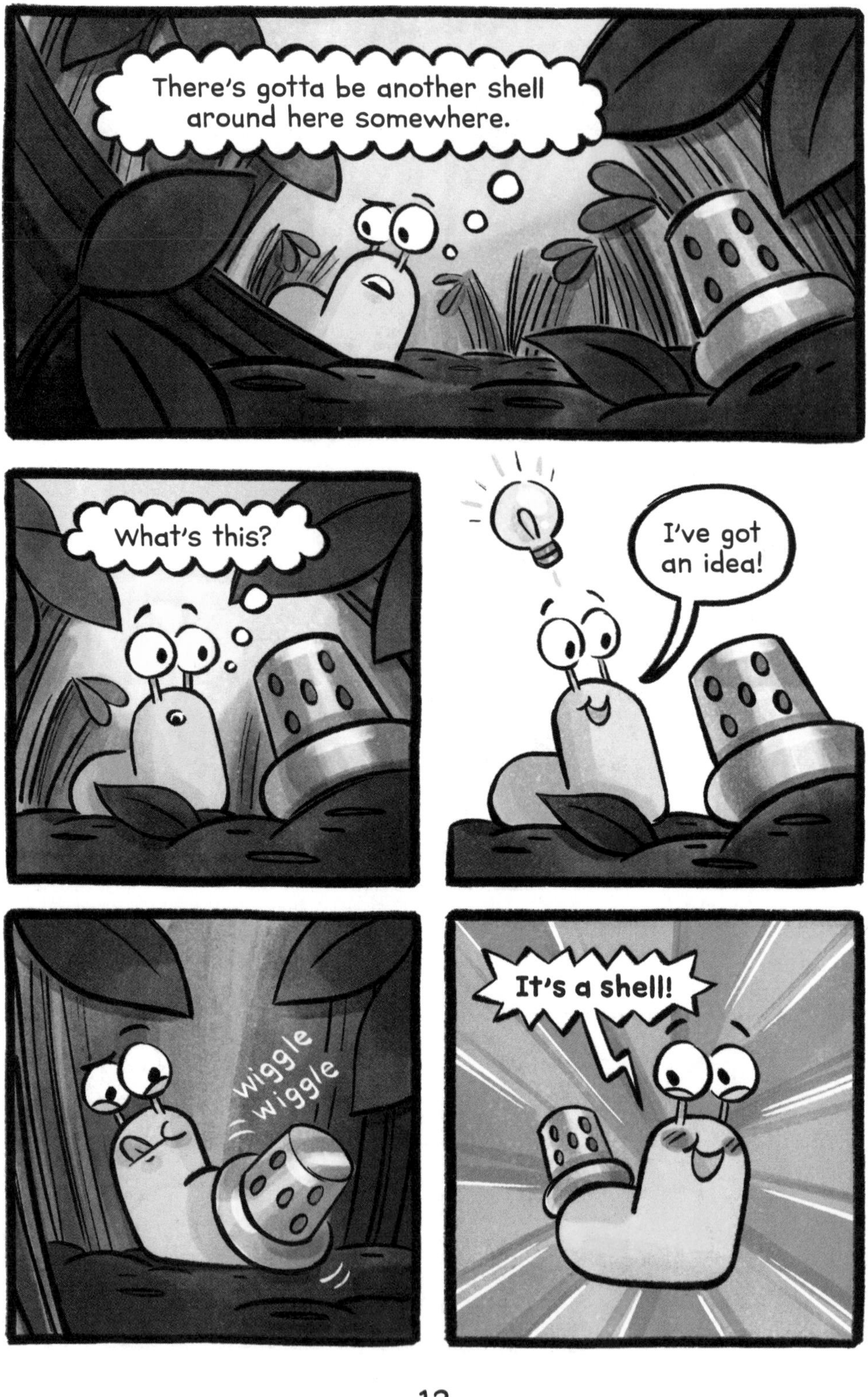
There's gotta be another shell around here somewhere.
What's this?
I've got an idea!
wiggle wiggle
It's a shell!

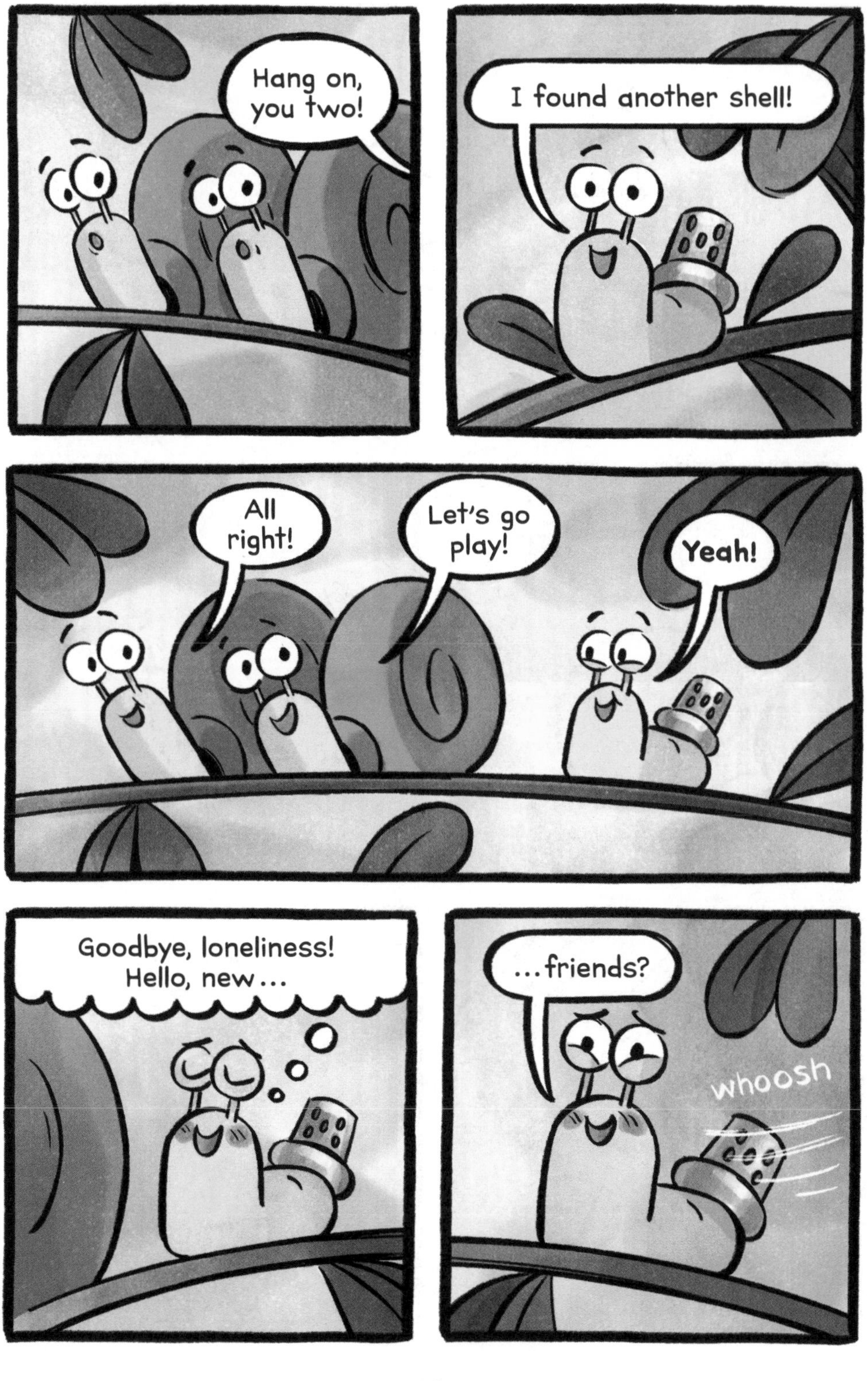
Hang on, you two!
I found another shell!
All right!
Let's go play!
Yeah!
Goodbye, loneliness! Hello, new...
...friends?
whoosh

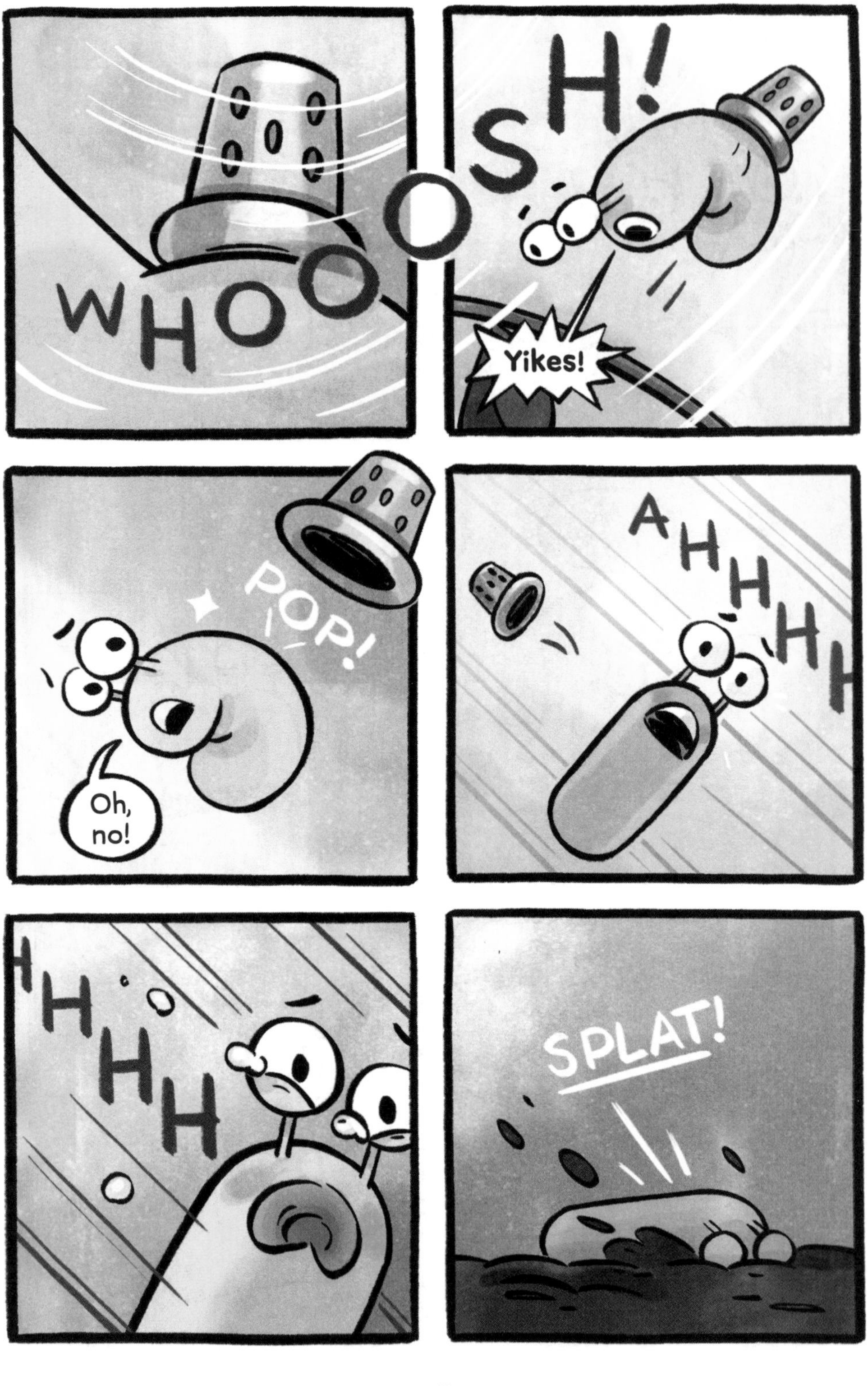
WHOOOSH!
Yikes!
POP!
Oh, no!
AHHHHHHHHH
SPLAT!

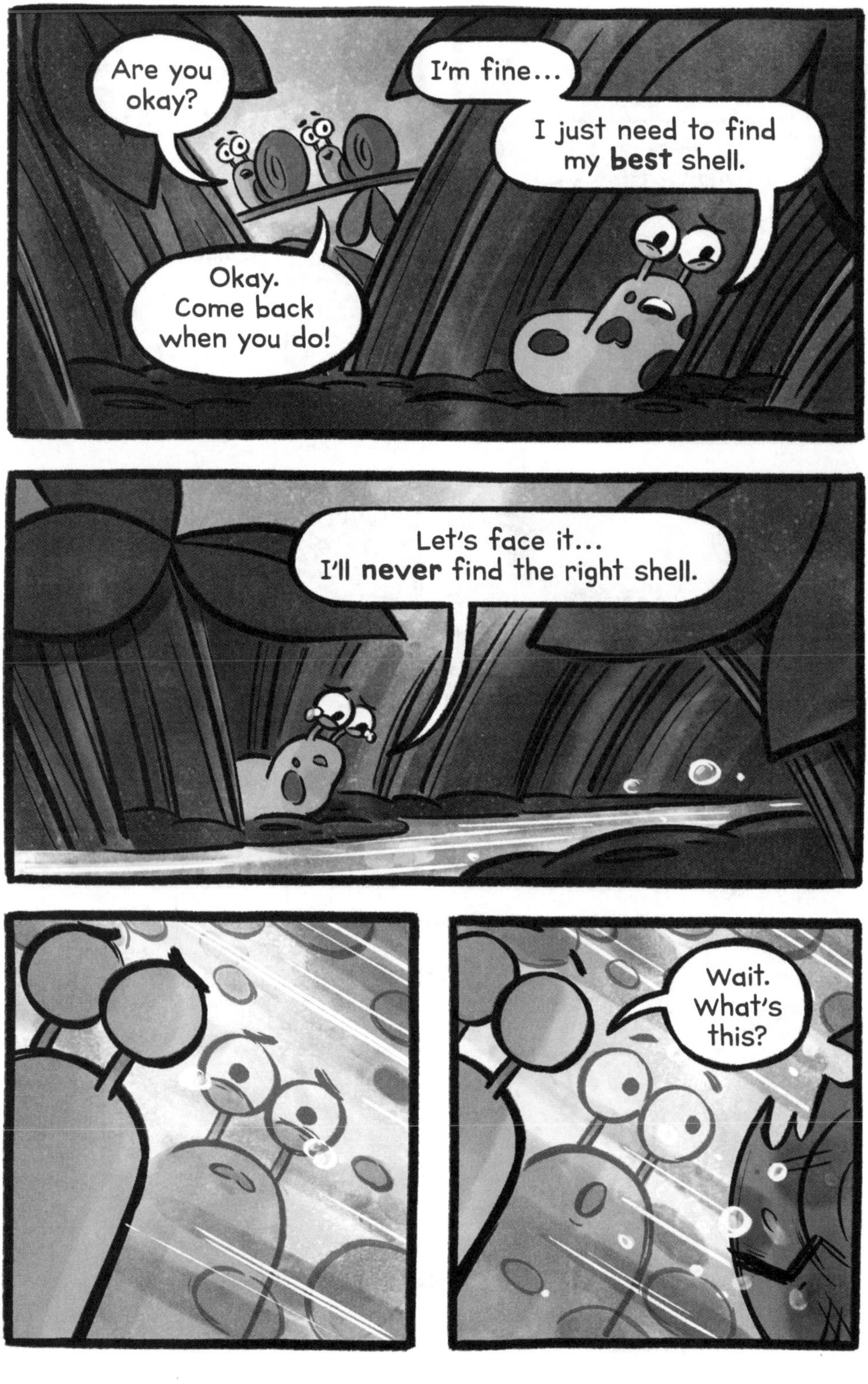
Are you okay?
I'm fine...
I just need to find my **best** shell.
Okay. Come back when you do!
Let's face it... I'll **never** find the right shell.
Wait. What's this?

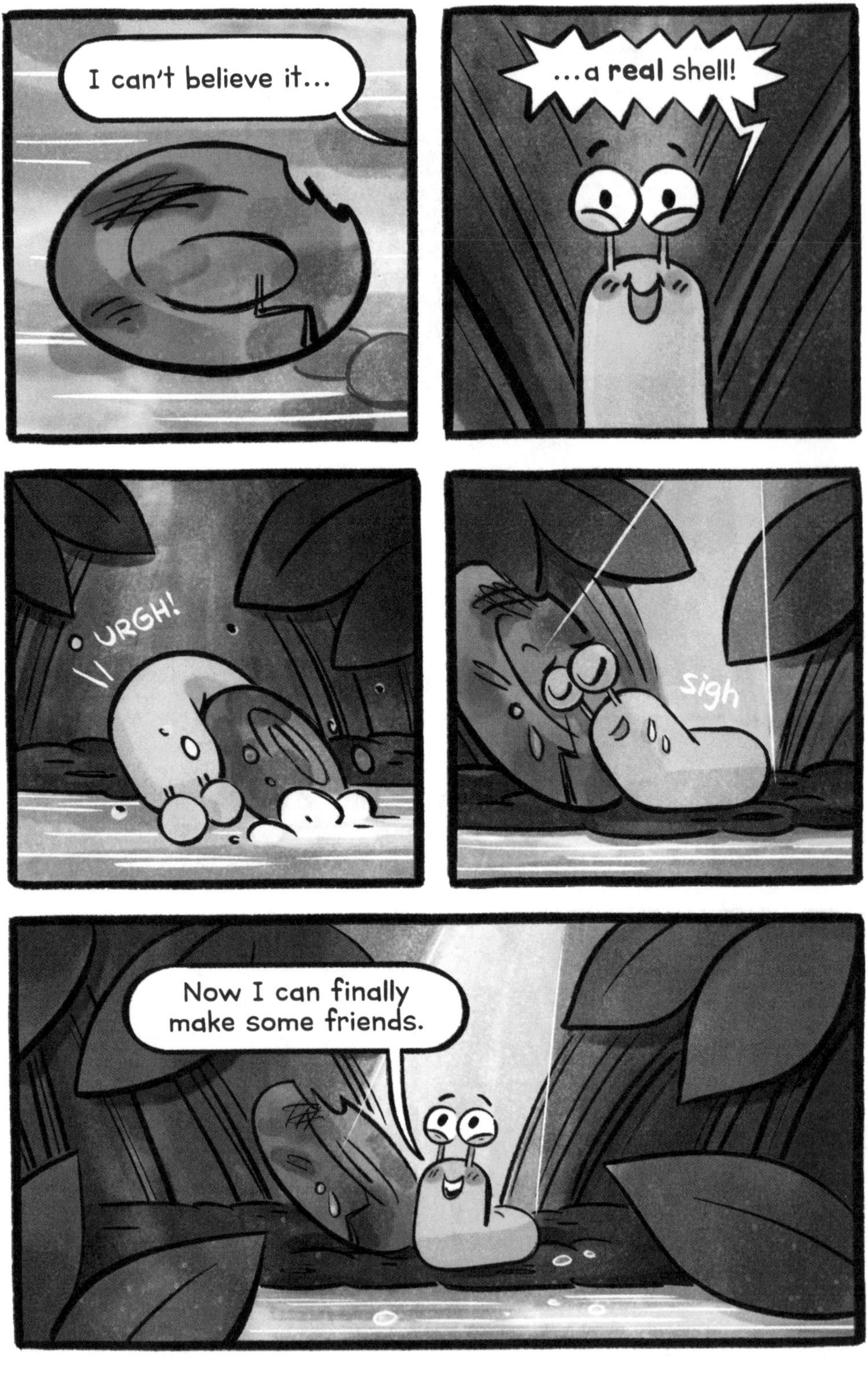
I can't believe it...
...a **real** shell!
URGH!
sigh
Now I can finally make some friends.

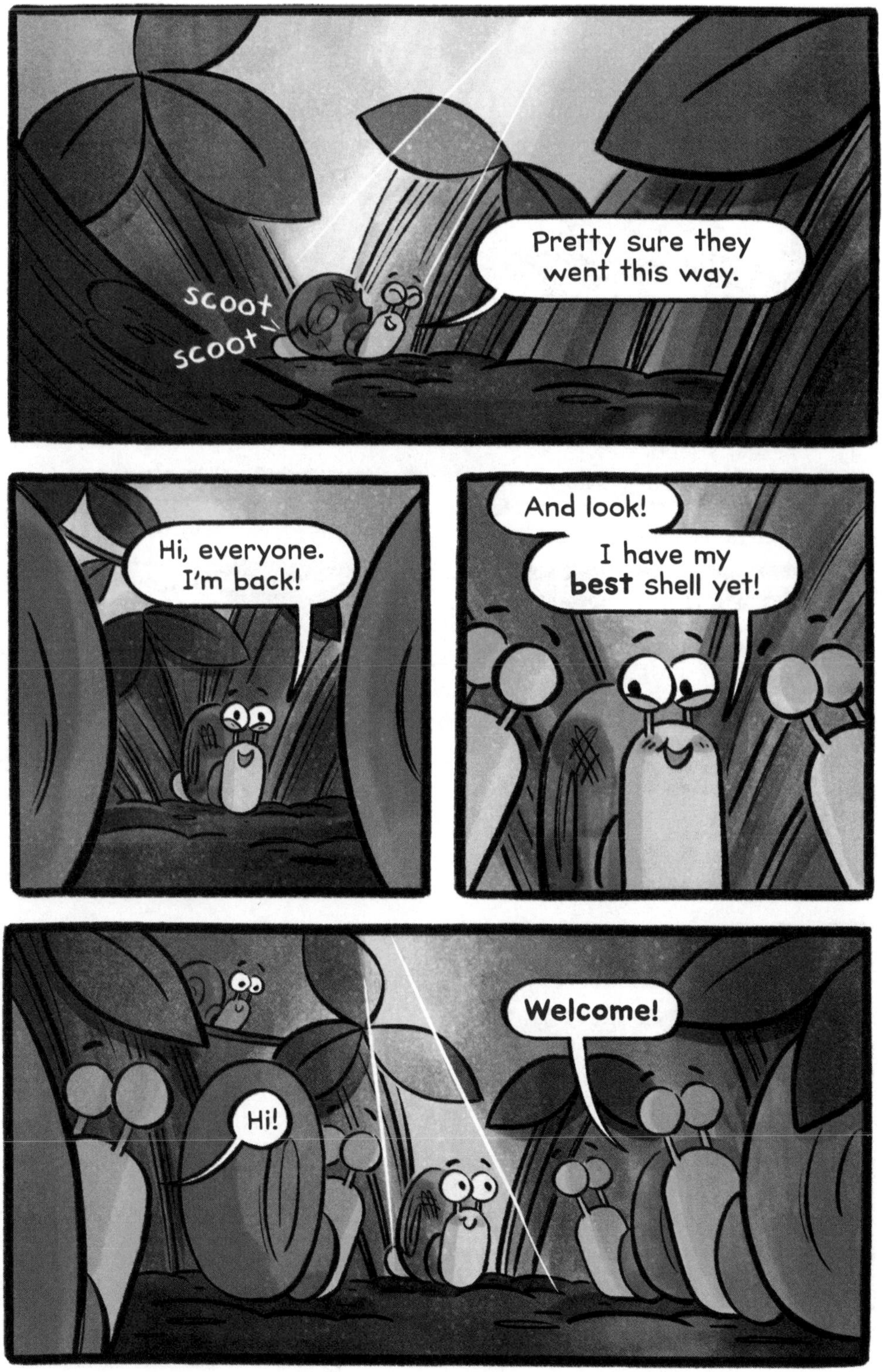
scoot
scoot
Pretty sure they went this way.
Hi, everyone. I'm back!
And look!
I have my **best** shell yet!
Hi!
Welcome!

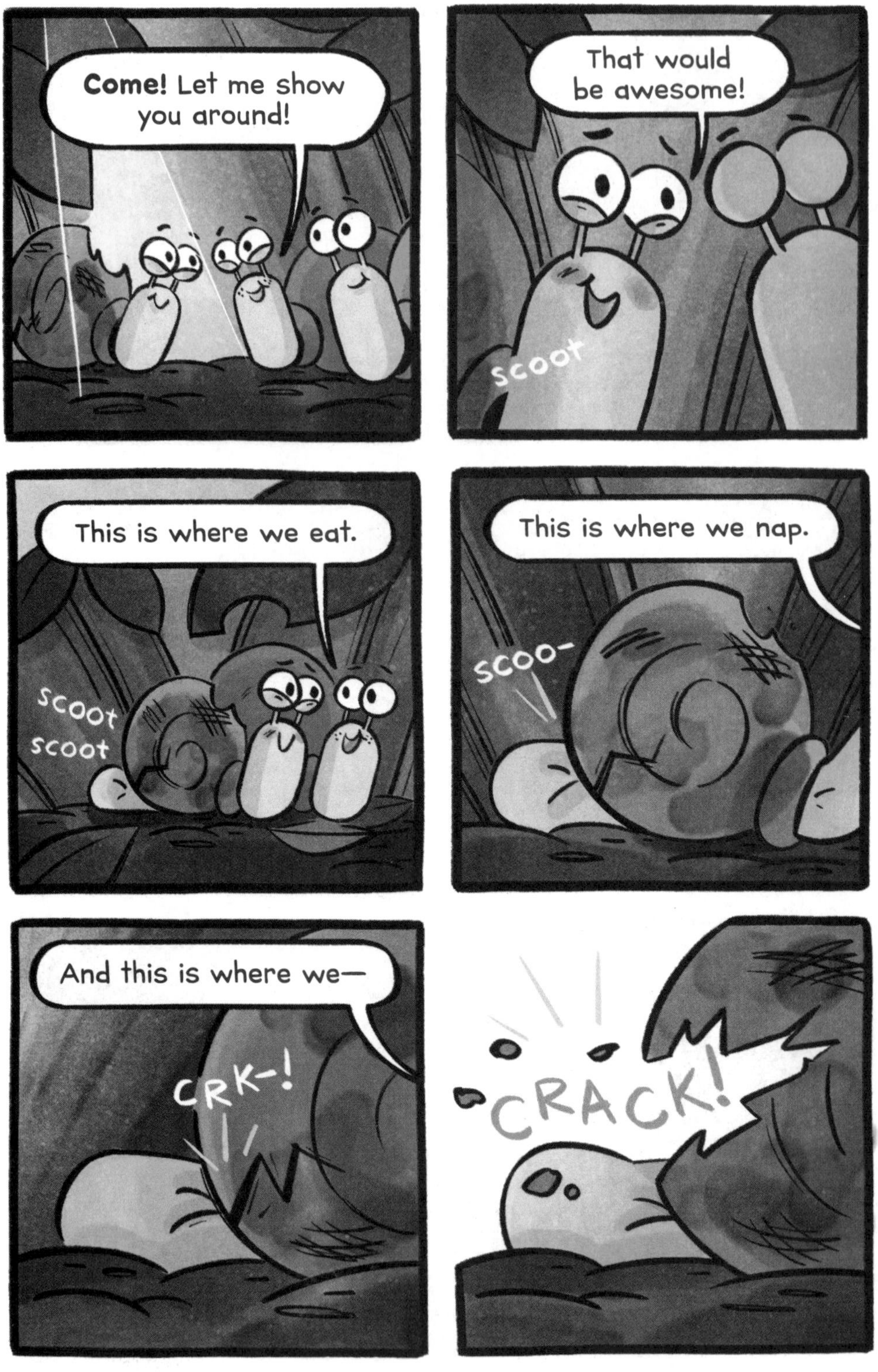

Come! Let me show you around!
That would be awesome!
scoot
This is where we eat.
scoot
scoot
This is where we nap.
scoo-
And this is where we—
CRK-!
CRACK!

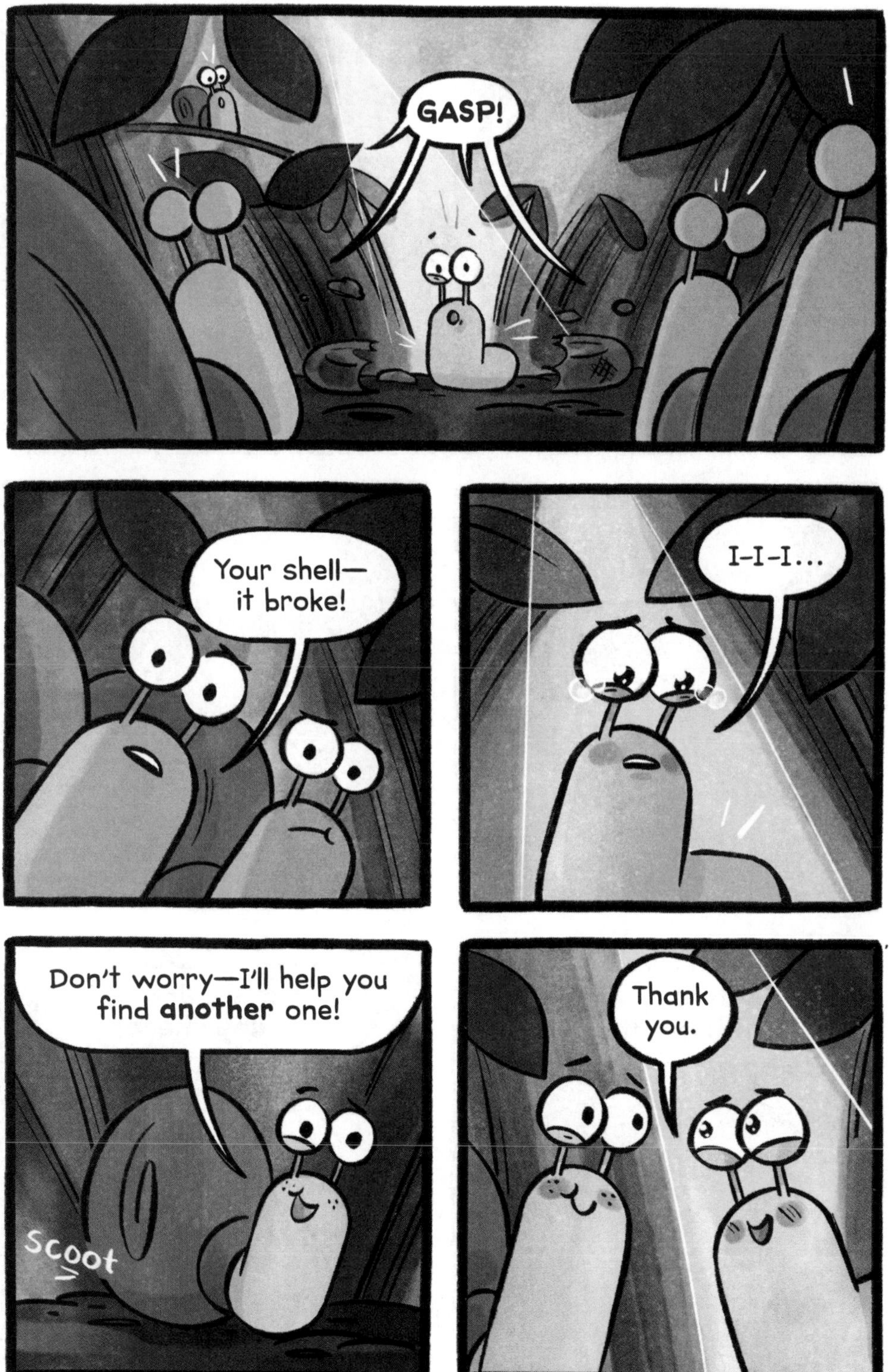
GASP!
Your shell—
it broke!
I-I-I...
Don't worry—I'll help you find **another** one!
scoot
Thank you.

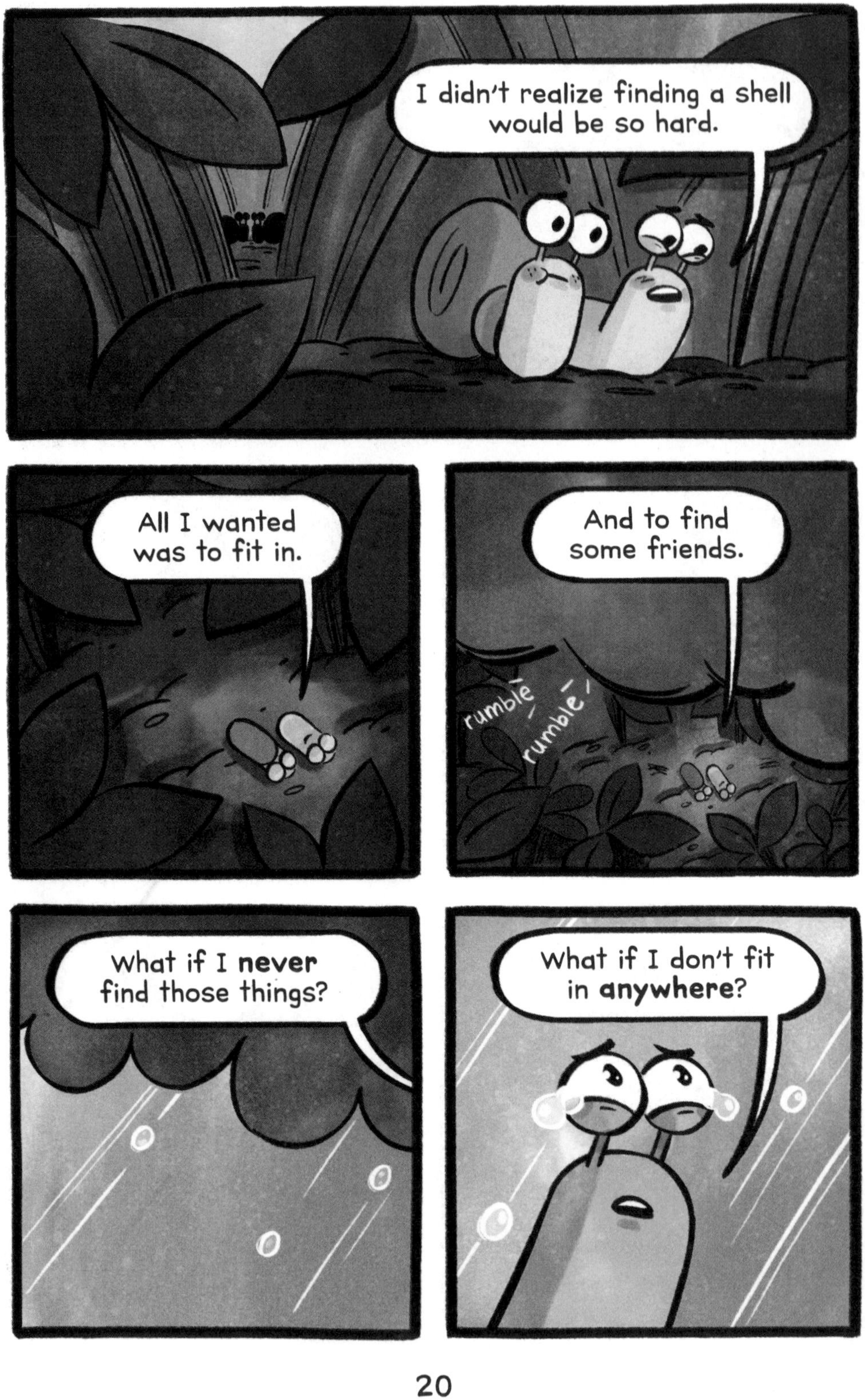
I didn't realize finding a shell would be so hard.
All I wanted was to fit in.
And to find some friends.
rumble rumble
What if I **never** find those things?
What if I don't fit in **anywhere**?

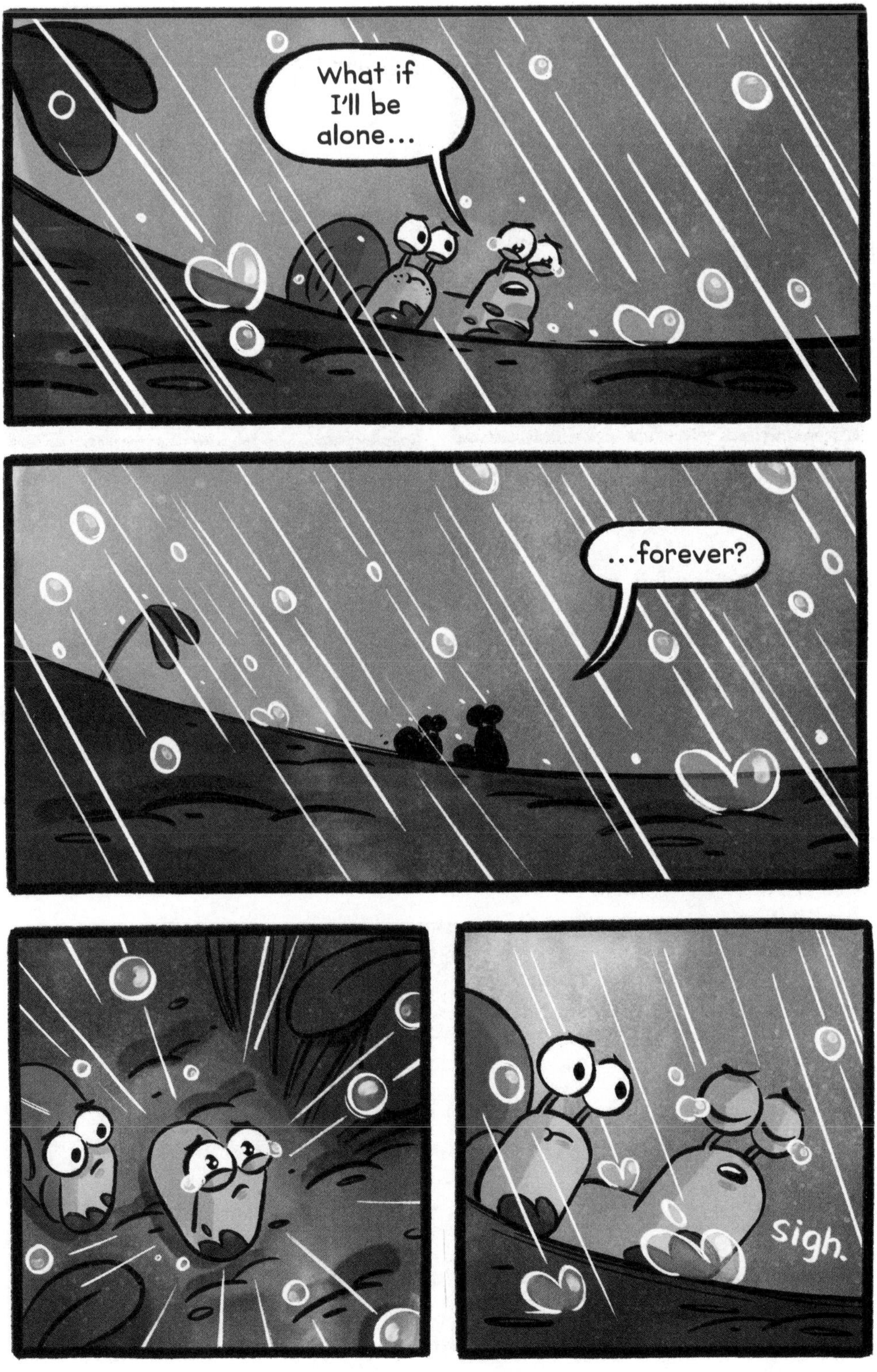
What if I'll be alone...
...forever?
Sigh.

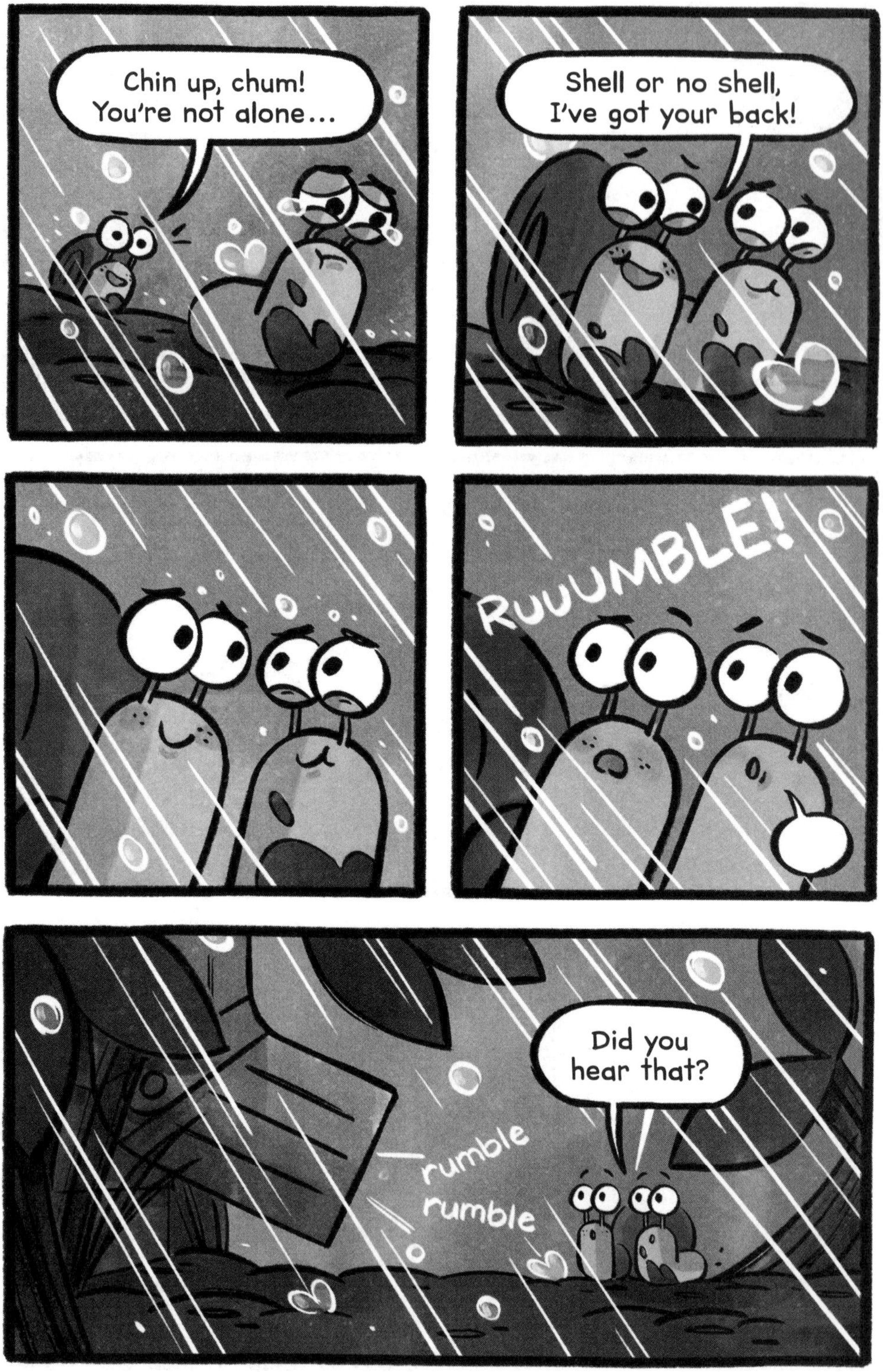
Chin up, chum!
You're not alone...
Shell or no shell,
I've got your back!
RUUUMBLE!
Did you
hear that?
rumble
rumble

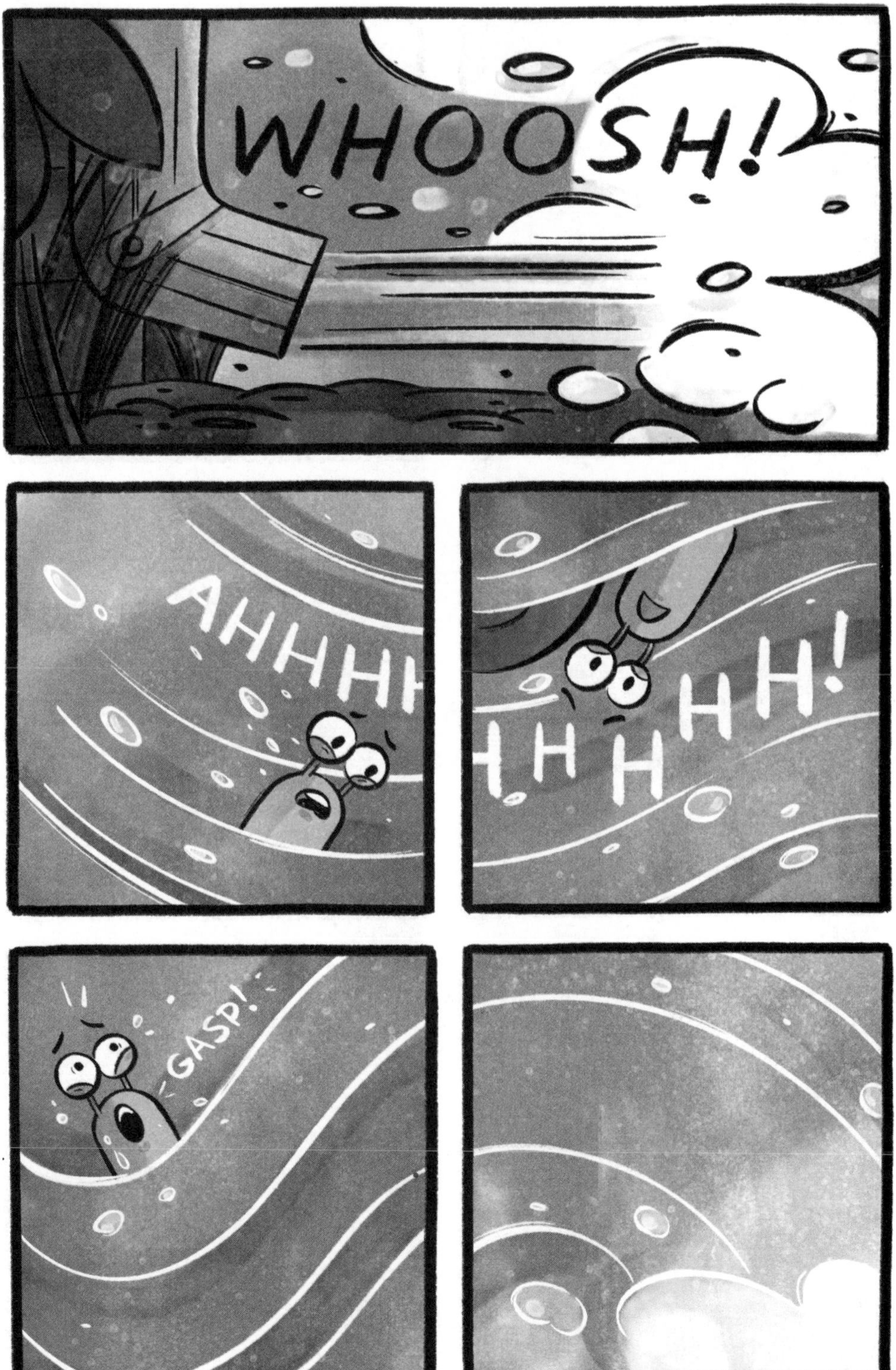
WHOOSH!
AHHHHHHHHHH!
GASP!

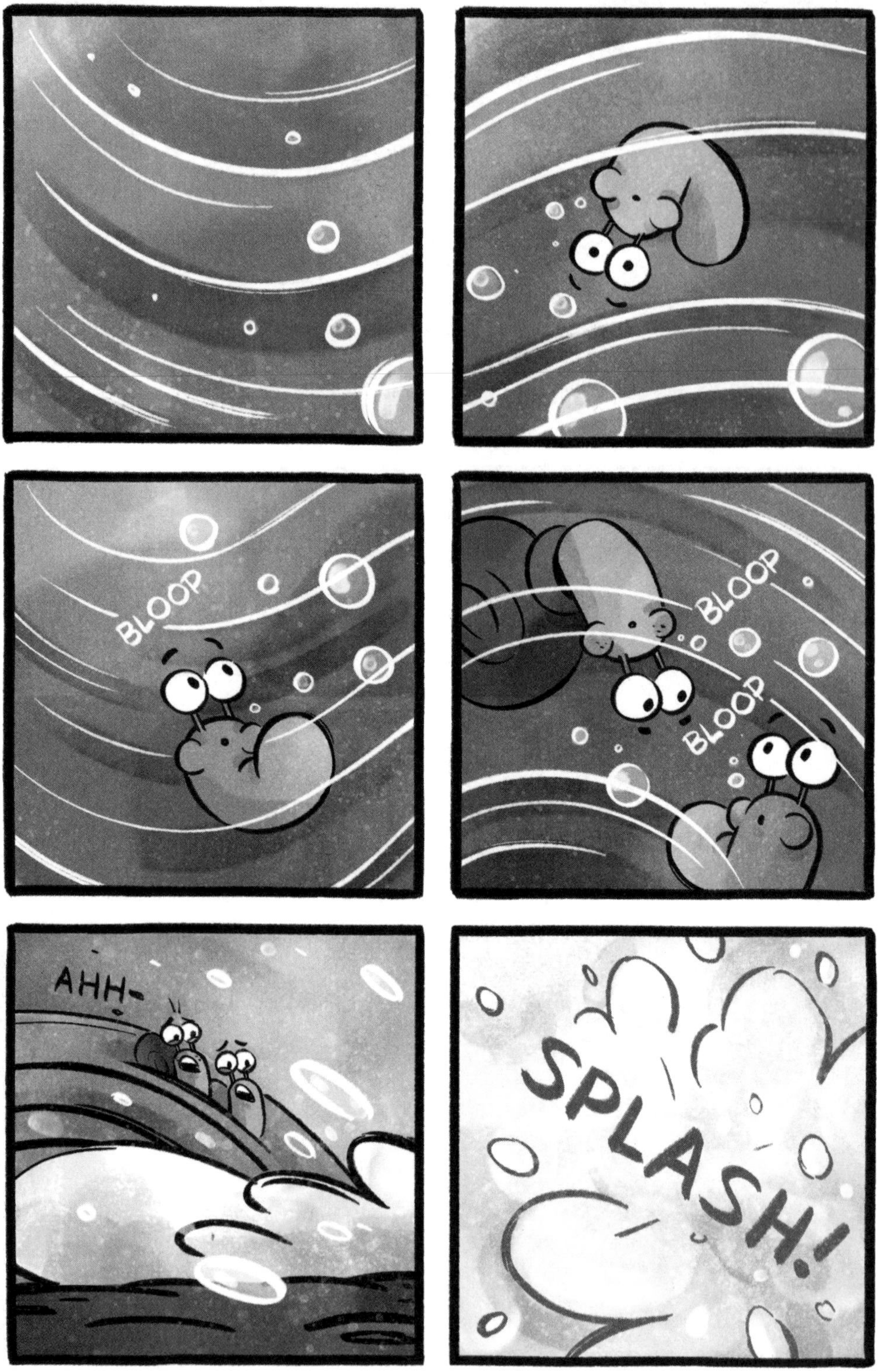
BLOOP
BLOOP
BLOOP
AHH-
SPLASH!

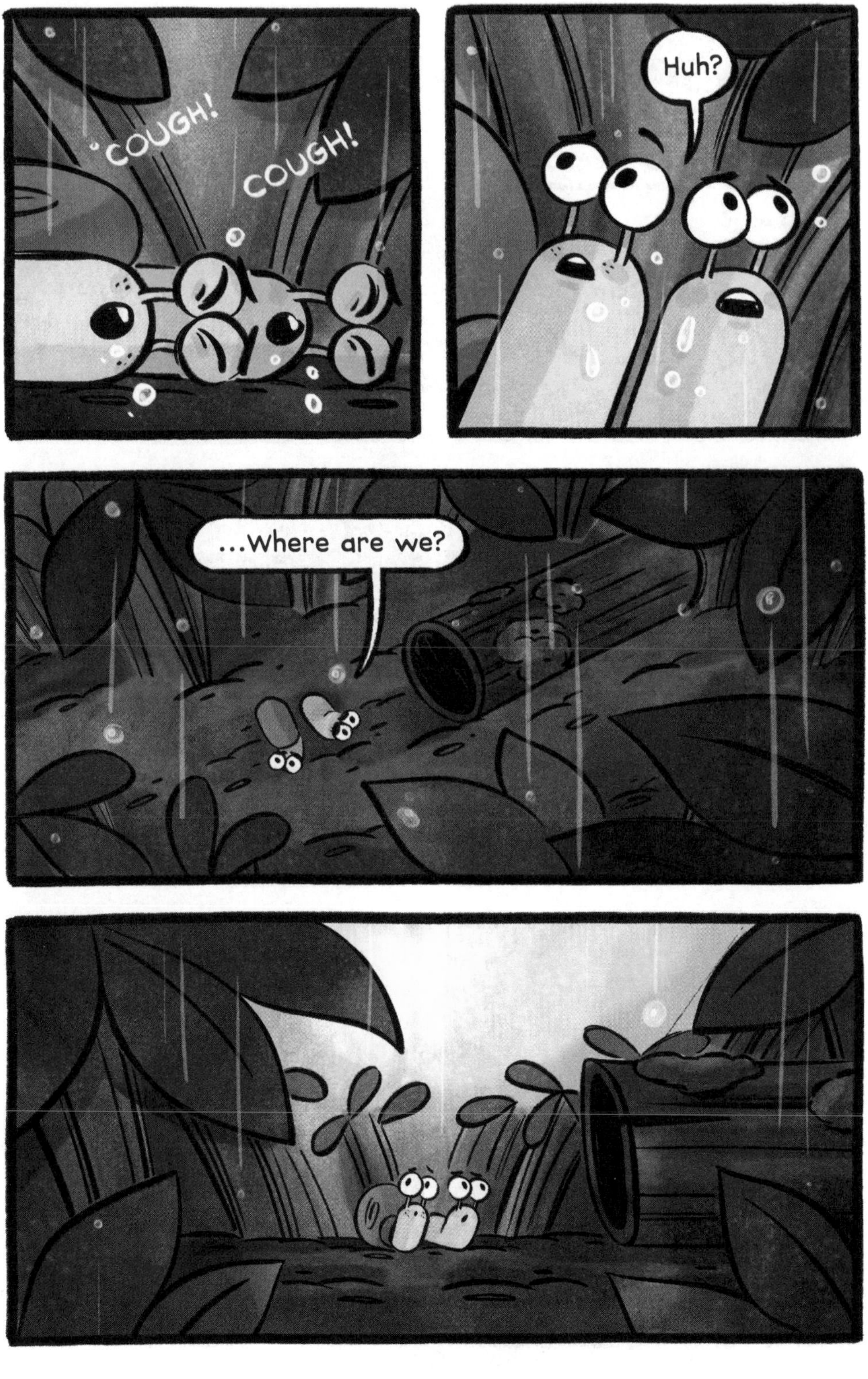
COUGH!
COUGH!
Huh?
...Where are we?

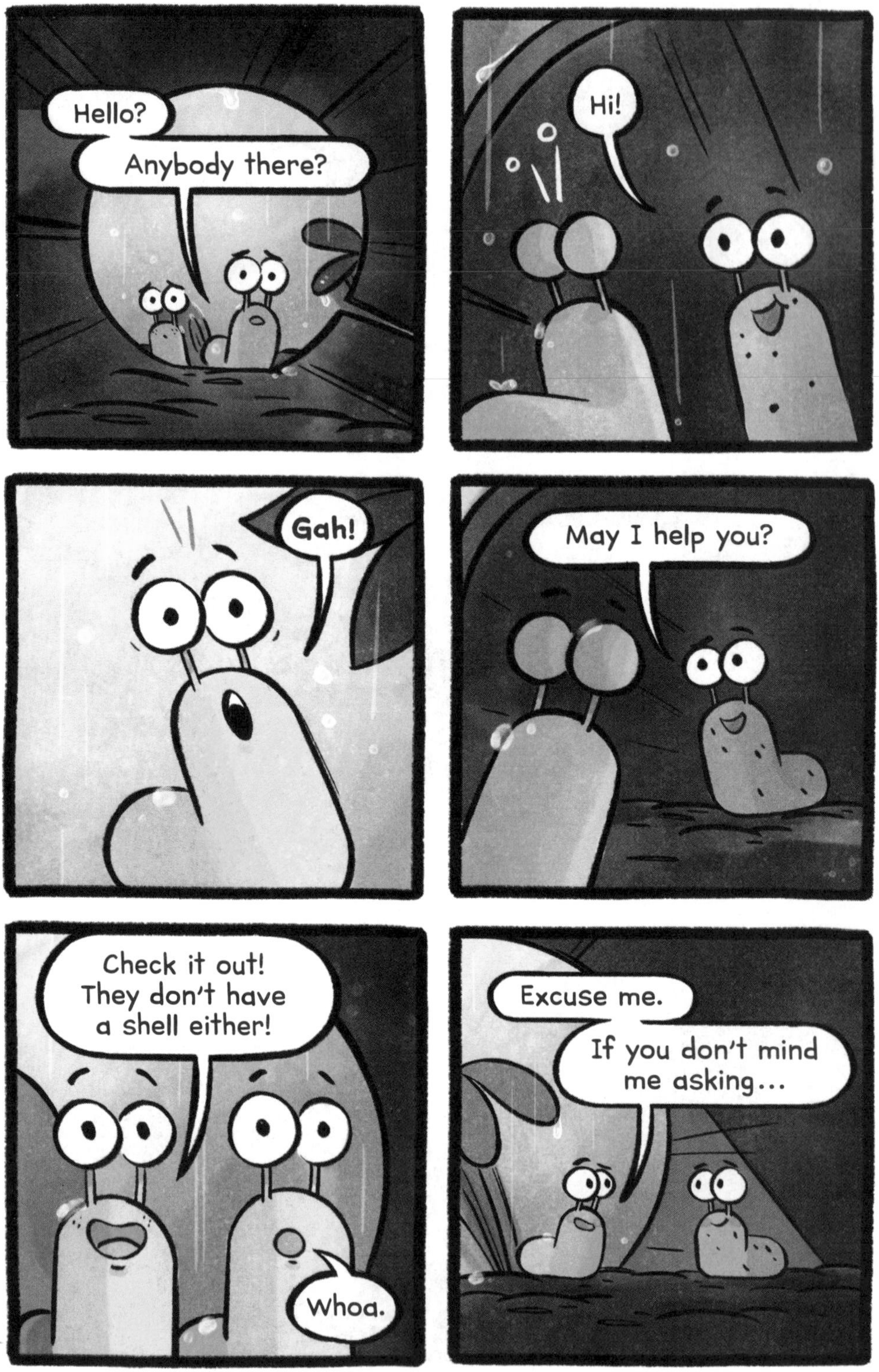
Hello?
Anybody there?
Hi!
Gah!
May I help you?
Check it out! They don't have a shell either!
Whoa.
Excuse me.
If you don't mind me asking...

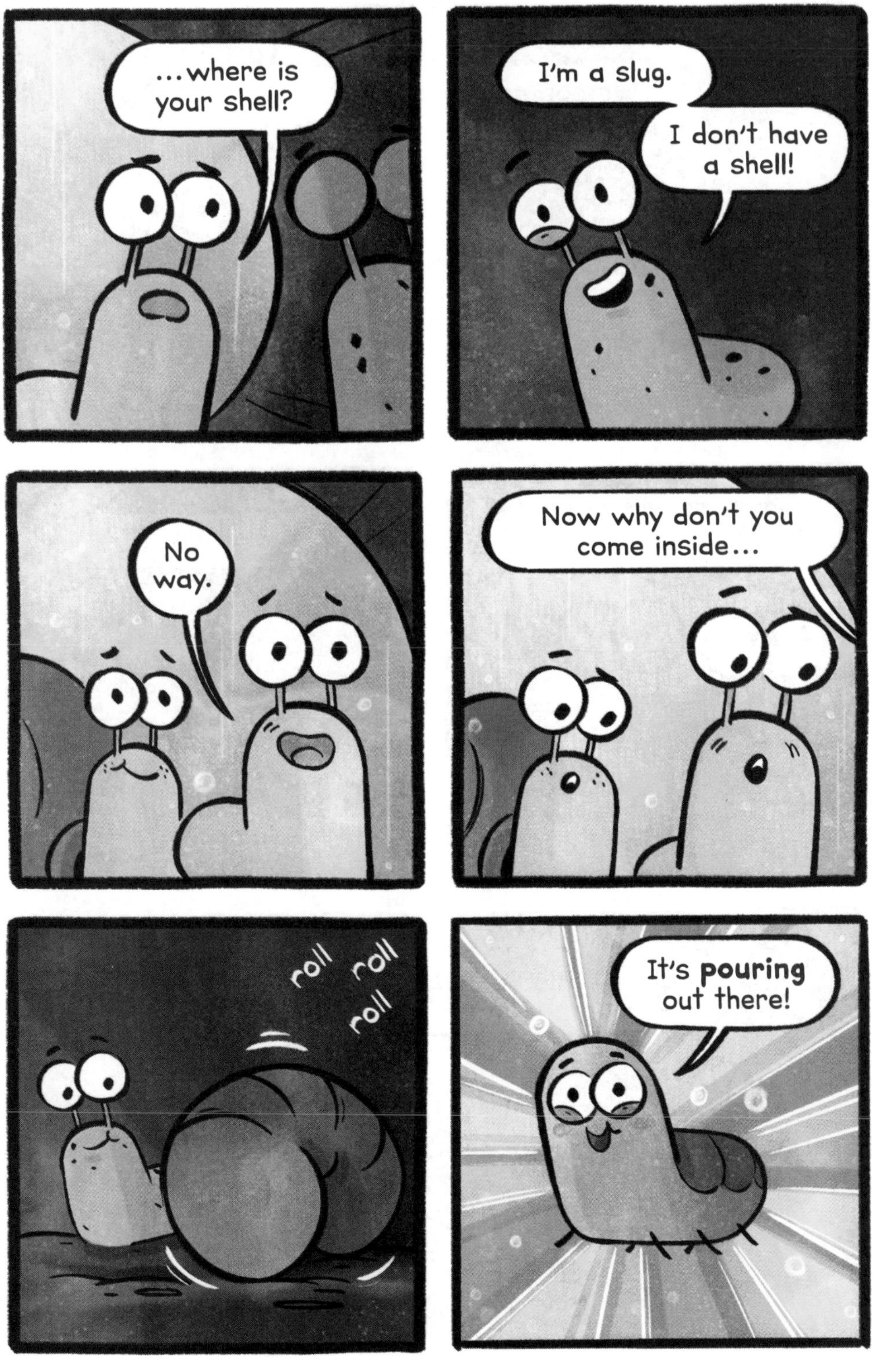
...where is your shell?
I'm a slug.
I don't have a shell!
No way.
Now why don't you come inside...
roll roll roll
It's **pouring** out there!

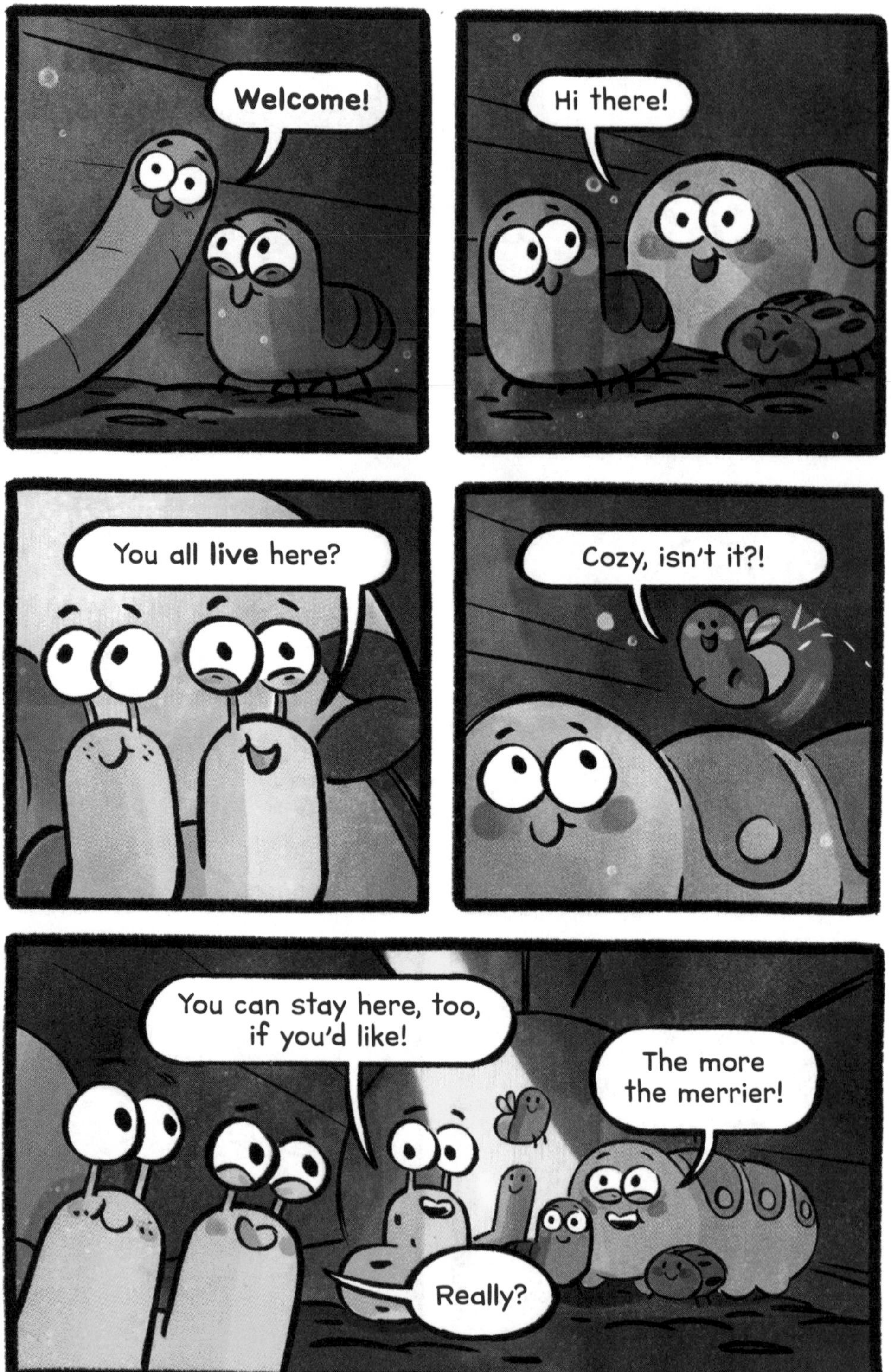
Welcome!
Hi there!
You all **live** here?
Cozy, isn't it?!
You can stay here, too, if you'd like!
The more the merrier!
Really?

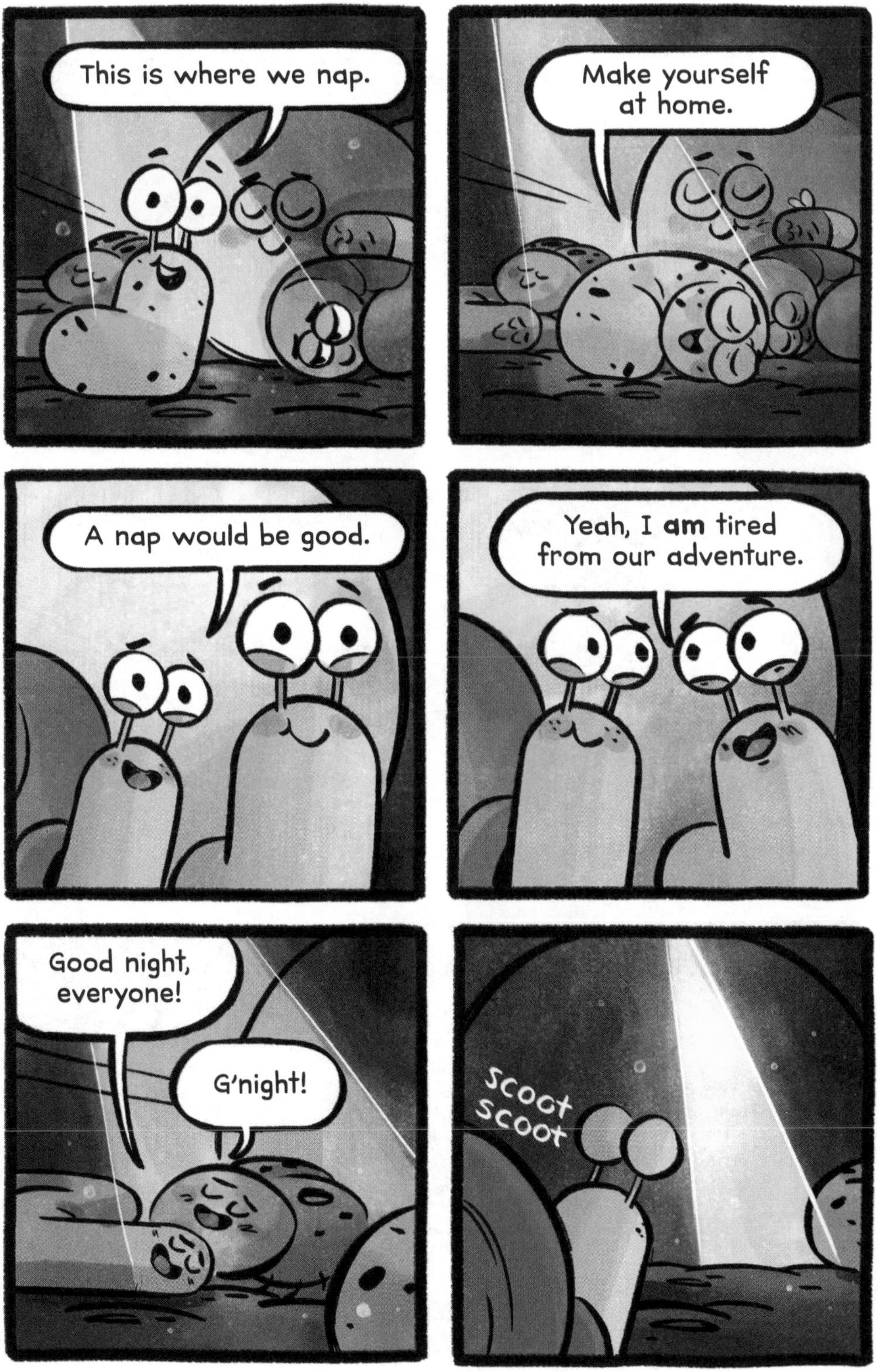
This is where we nap.
Make yourself at home.
A nap would be good.
Yeah, I **am** tired from our adventure.
Good night, everyone!
G'night!
SCOOT SCOOT

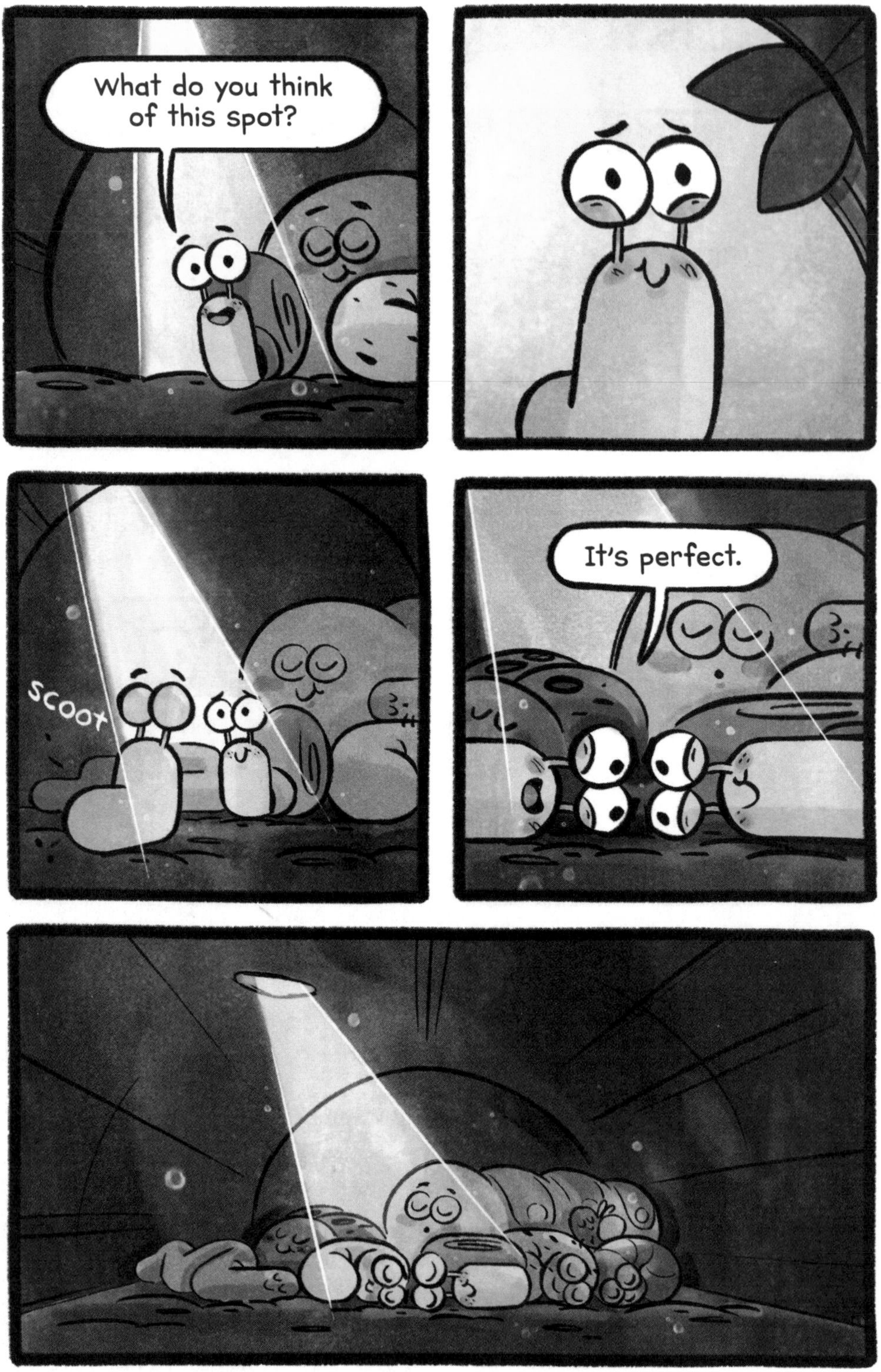
What do you think of this spot?
SCOOT
It's perfect.

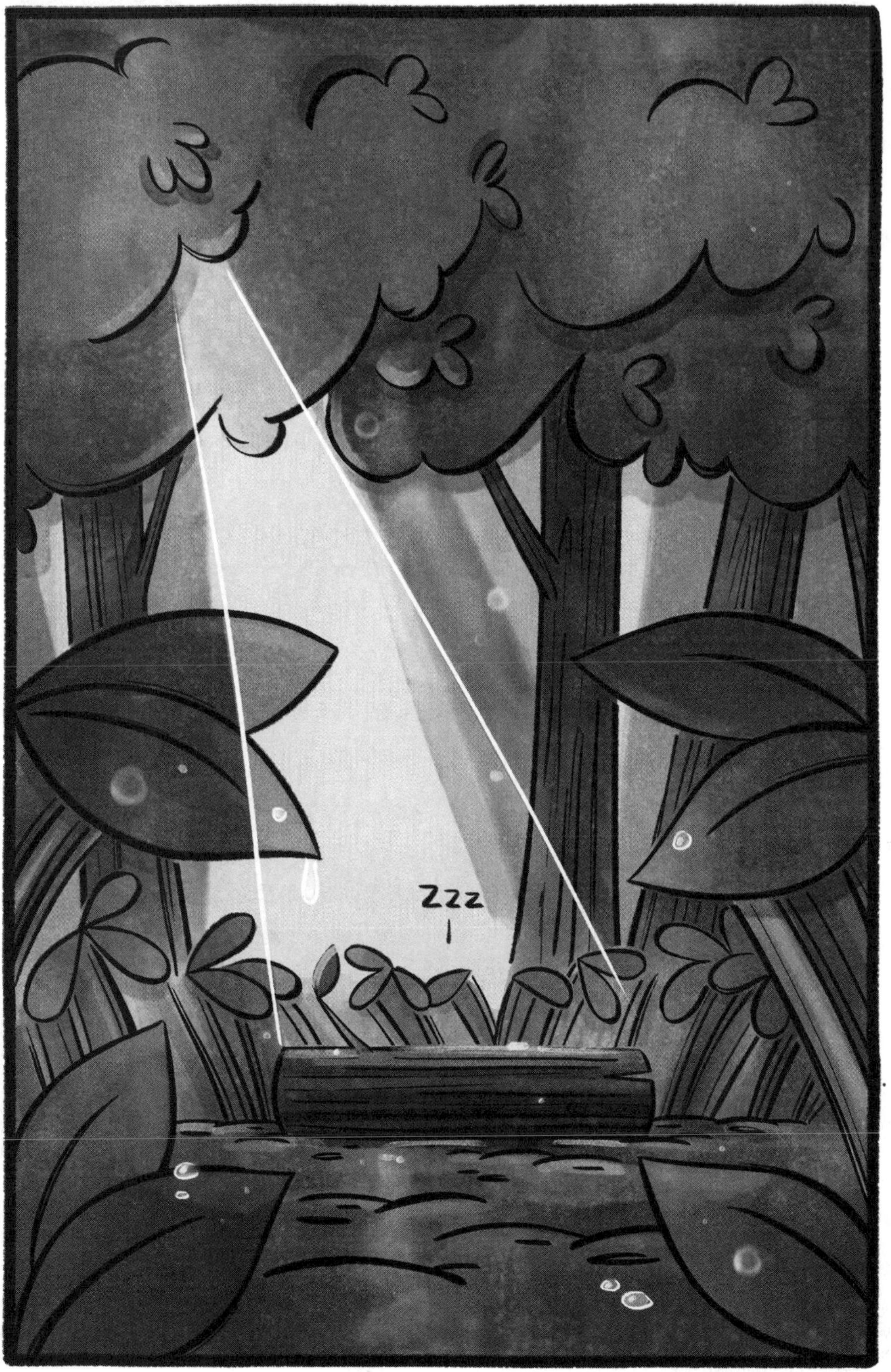
Zzz

A NATURE GUIDE
SLUG (VS) SNAIL

- Land slugs grow up to 10 inches (25.4cm).
- Slugs have no visible shell and live under loose bark, stones, and logs.
- Most slugs live up to 6 years in the wild.

- Land snails vary greatly in size, from under an inch up to 12 inches or more.
- Snails have shells on their backs.
- Most land snails live 2 to 3 years in the wild, but some can live more than 10.

Both are called **gastropods**, which comes from the Greek word **gastros**, meaning **stomach**, and **podos**, meaning **foot**.

For more information on slugs and snails, check out: kids.nationalgeographic.com, kids.britannica.com, and carnegiemnh.org.

"stomach foot"